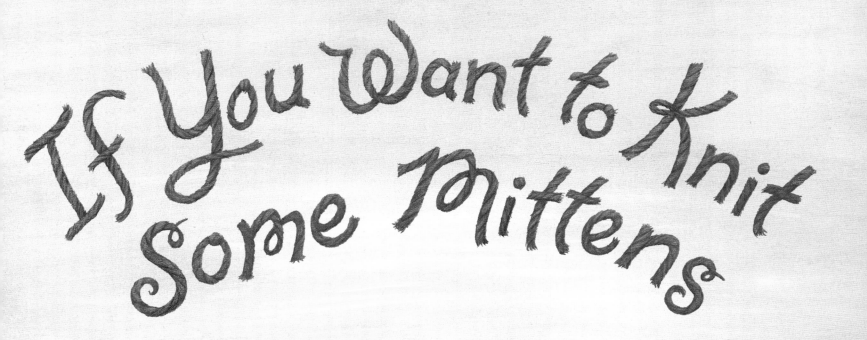

If You Want to Knit Some Mittens

Illustrated by

Laura Purdie Salas   Angela Matteson

BOYDS MILLS PRESS

AN IMPRINT OF BOYDS MILLS & KANE

New York

With love for my mom, Dorothy Purdie;
my mom-in-law, Noella Salas; my grandma Dorothy Foshée;
and all who show love by creating with needles,
yarn, thread, and fabric
—*LPS*

For Mom and Dad, who have always encouraged
my creative endeavors
—*AM*

*Acknowledgments: With gratitude to Christa Rochford
of the American Wool Council, and with thanks to Susan Gesch
of Fleecewood Farm in Hastings, Minnesota,
for introducing me to the joy of spring lambs.*
—LPS

This book is designed to provide humorous information on the subjects discussed.
It should not be used or viewed as an instruction guide or manual—yes, even if you
have your very own pet sheep. The publisher, author, and illustrator are not responsible
for any injury that may result from following the suggestions made in this book and
are not liable for any damages or negative consequences from any treatment, action,
application, or preparation to any person (or sheep) reading or following the suggestions
or information in this book. We want you (and ewe) to be safe!

For information about permission to reproduce selections from this book,
please contact permissions@bmkbooks.com.

Boyds Mills Press
An imprint of Boyds Mills & Kane, a division of Astra Publishing House
boydsmillspress.com
Printed in China

ISBN: 978-1-62979-564-5 (hc) • 978-1-63592-465-7 (eBook)
Library of Congress Control Number: 2020947626

First edition
10 9 8 7 6 5 4 3 2 1

Design by Anahid Hamparian
The text is set in Aleo.
The illustrations were painted with acrylics, gouache,
and a touch of colored pencil on wood board.

1. Get a sheep.

2. Keep her warm and well fed
through the long, chilly winter.

Wish for mittens.
Wait for spring.

3. In spring, your sheep might beg
for a mohawk or for pig—no, *sheep*tails.

But scraggly sheep need a neat, complete buzz cut.

4. Soak the dirty fleece in soapy water.
Rinse out grass and food and dirt.
Sheep are not the cleanest creatures.

"No offense meant, Sheep.
A barn is not the
cleanest place."

5. Gently press the fleece to squeeze out the water.

Riding your bike over it does not work.

6. Once it's dry, pick the fleece into pieces.
Then, use bristly paddles to card them.
This untangles the fibers.

It does not work
on people hair!

7. Spin your wispy wool into yarn.
Let your spinning wheel *hummm* and
sing your sheep to sleep.

8. Choose a color for your mittens.

Sunny gold? Great!
But chances are your sheep
did not grow gold wool!

9. Quick—plant some marigolds.
You need soil. Sun. Water.

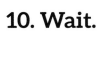

12. Wait.

Well, nobody said this would be a quick project!

13. Pick marigolds and dry them in the sun.

Jumping rope nearby is
not recommended.

14. Make an icky mixture and soak your yarn in it. This step helps the dye stick better later.

It only *looks* like noodle soup.

Remove the noo—yarn and rinse it off.

15. Soak your marigolds in water.

"It's marigold magic, Sheep!"

16. Cook your yarn in the marigold dye.

17. Then spread your yarn out to dry.

You might think it would make a cool mummy costume.

It would not.

18. Get some knitting needles and learn to knit.
Let your fingers fly. *Click-clack! Slip-snip!*
Knit your mittens.

Wait for winter.

Whew. Now slip on your mittens.
Hold the golden sun in your hands.

Have a warm and woolly winter
with your friend Sheep.